I0715239

THE STORY OF SIR FRANCIS DRAKE

This edition published 2025
by Living Book Press
Copyright © Living Book Press, 2025

ISBN: 978-1-76153-551-2 (hardcover)
         978-1-76153-558-1 (softcover)

First published in 1906.

All rights reserved. No part of this publication may be reproduced, stored in a retrieval system, or transmitted in any other form or means – electronic, mechanical, photocopying, recording or otherwise, without the prior permission of the copyright owner and the publisher or as provided by Australian law.

A catalogue record for this book is available from the National Library of Australia

THE STORY OF SIR FRANCIS DRAKE

by

OLIVER ELTON

LIVING BOOK
PRESS

GET ALL OF THE 'HISTORY SHAPERS' BOOKS
The Story of...

David Livingstone	Robert Bruce	Chalmers of New
H. M. Stanley	General Gordon	Guinea
Abraham Lincoln	Lord Clive	Bishop Patteson
Sir Francis Drake	Captain Cook	Joan of Arc
Sir Walter Raleigh	Nelson	Napoleon
Columbus	Lord Roberts	Cromwell

PLEASE NOTE

In this series, you will read about historical figures who displayed courage, bravery, self-sacrifice, and many other admirable traits. Their stories remind us that many people in history took bold actions and made tough choices. Yet, even those who achieved great things sometimes held ideas or pursued goals that were not beneficial to everyone. History is full of complex individuals—parts of their lives inspire us to be brave and stand up for what is right, while other parts remind us to consider the unintended consequences of our actions.

As you explore these biographies, we invite you to reflect on the qualities that enabled these figures to achieve greatness and the lessons we can learn from their mistakes. Maybe you too can become a History Shaper—someone who learns from the past and helps to make our world a better place for everyone.

Contents

Philip of Spain

During the life of Francis Drake, Philip the Second of Spain was the most powerful king in Europe. Spain and the Netherlands belonged to him, parts of Italy, France, and Germany, and a great part of America. From Mexico, Peru, and the West Indian Islands, Spanish ships sailed home with treasure of silver and gold, as they do in fairy tales, while Portuguese ships traded in Africa for slaves and gold and ivory, and had even ventured as far as the then little-known East Indies. Lastly, Philip added Portugal and its possessions to his vast inheritance, and would have liked to hold all the world "for God and for Spain." Being himself a good Catholic, he wished to see all men of that faith, and to those who did not believe in it he was a merciless foe, and he shed the blood of many martyrs.

Now Drake hated Philip and the Pope more than anything in the world, as much as he loved England and honoured his own Queen Elizabeth. He spent most of his life in making war against the King of Spain in one way or another, calling it all, as he told Queen Elizabeth, "service done to your Majesty by your poor vassal (or servant) against your great enemy."

During Drake's life wars about religion were raging in

almost every European country. In France the struggle ended by most people remaining Catholics, just as England, after Elizabeth's reign, was always a Protestant country. But such changes really take long to come about, especially in days when news travelled slowly, when there were no trains or steamships, and no penny newspapers.

Francis Drake was born when Edward the Sixth was king, in a farmhouse near Tavistock in Devonshire; but while he was quite a young child his father, who was a Protestant, had to fly from his country home, owing to an outbreak of anger among his Catholic neighbours. So the first stories the little Francis would hear must have been tales of this time of persecution, when many of his father's friends had to hide in woods and caves, and lost all they possessed. From his very cradle he must have been taught to hate the "Papists."

The new home was rather a strange one, for the old books say Drake's father went to Kent, "to inhabit in the hull of a ship, wherein many of his younger sons were born. He had twelve in all, and as it pleased God that most of them should be born upon the water, so the greater part of them died at sea. "The father seems to have been a sailor at one time, and he now got a place among the seamen of the King's Navy, to read prayers to them. The Navy ships were anchored off Chatham when not in use, and here, in an old unused warship, the elder Drake and his family made their floating home. Here most of the twelve boys were born, a troop of merry children, and many a fine game they must have had on the decks.

The sound of wind and waves must have been familiar to them as they went to sleep at nights, and they grew up strong and fearless, and, living as they did among sailors, must have early set their hearts on going to sea and having adventures.

At the death of King Edward the Sixth, the Catholic Queen Mary began to reign, and Philip, then Prince of Spain, came over to marry her. He looked "very gallant," they said, in his suit of white kid, covered with gold embroidery, and was followed by a train of splendid-looking Spanish nobles, and he brought quantities of gold and silver, borne on the backs of horses. But the English people hated the foreign marriage, and so strong was this feeling that in the winter before the wedding even the children in the streets shouted against the Spaniards and snowballed them as they went to Court. Perhaps Francis Drake and his brothers left their usual games to play at being Philip and the English, like some other lads, of whom we read that their play became so real and exciting that they were only just prevented from hanging the boy who acted the part of Philip. The King of Spain might have seen his son upon the English throne, but this hope, like so many of his, was doomed to be defeated, for Mary died childless, and Elizabeth came to the throne.

As Drake's father was at this time a poor man, he put his son Francis to learn seamanship of the master of a bark or small ship that used to coast along the shore and sometimes carried merchandise to France and the Netherlands. At this time he must have had to suffer many hardships and to live a rough life, but he learned his business well, and "was so diligent and painstaking, and so pleased the old man his master by his industry," that at his death he left his bark to Francis Drake.

Later Drake grew weary of this little ship, that "only crept along the shore," and longed for something more than such safe and simple voyaging, so he seems to have sold the bark and taken service with his kinsmen, the Hawkins brothers, who were rich merchants and owned and sailed their ships. And so began Drake's roving life.

"The Troublesome Voyage"

The four centuries before the sixteenth, in which Drake lived, have been called the Age of Discovery. The world widened before men's eyes as new lands and seas, new peoples, and even new stars, became known to them. The little country of Portugal was the first to begin those discoveries. Her ships explored the coasts of Africa and traded there. One of her mariners discovered the passage round the Cape of Good Hope to India, the Spice Islands, and China, and for long she had no rival in her trade.

About fifty years before Drake was born, America was discovered by Christopher Columbus, an Italian sailor in the service of Spain. The ships in use in those days were very different to any we see now. There have been three kinds of ships made, ships with oars, ships with sails, and ships with steam. They are divided into two kinds, fighting ships and merchant ships.

The old-fashioned galley was long and low-decked, and could be rowed or sailed. In the middle of the ship, between two platforms or upper decks, the rowers were chained to their seats. Three or four men worked each of the long oars, or sweeps as they were called. There were twenty-five oars or more on each side of the ship. The rowers or galley-slaves were generally prisoners taken in war, and to "be sent to the galleys" was a terrible fate. They lived on the benches, ill-fed and ill-clothed, with only an awning to cover them when in port, though the low sides of the ships protected them a little from the weather and from the fire of the enemy. Drake seems always to have released the slaves he took on Spanish galleys. Once, we are told, they included "Turks, Greeks, Negroes, Frenchmen, and Spaniards."

The sailors who worked the ships were free. The ships were always armed, at first with shields and spears and arrows, later with guns and powder. With such ships the Italians fought many great battles on the Mediterranean, and in such ships, the Norsemen had invaded England and raided the Northern Seas; and, with his *caravels*, or light Spanish ships, Columbus reached the islands which he called the West Indies. In later voyages he reached the mainland of America, but to the day of his death he always believed that he had found the coast of Asia. Another Italian sailor, named Amerigo, also in the service of Spain, gave his name to the New World. The Italians had long been good sailors and ship-builders, and great fighters at sea, and they had the glory of discovering America, though they gained no possessions there.

Spain, at that time the most powerful state in Europe, seized upon a great part of the new land, and found there gold and silver mines. The natives they first subdued and afterwards forced to become Christians, as the custom was in warfare with a Pagan race.

The American Indians, however, have never been easy to subdue, and have always had an undying affection for their own way of life. The Spaniards found them unfitted for hard work in the mines. The Portuguese had already captured negroes in their West African settlements, and numbers of those were sent to America as slaves.

From the time of Henry the Eighth the English were building and buying fine ships, and learnt to sail them so well that they began less and less to use the old galley ship with its many oars. They traded mostly with Spain and the Low Countries; but as they got better ships, and became expert sailors, they wanted to go farther away, to discover new countries and get more trade. They began to sail to the Canary Islands, to Africa, and America.

The Hawkins family had taken a large part in this new activity. The elder William Hawkins had sailed to Brazil; and his son, John Hawkins, with whom Drake took service, made several voyages to the "Isles of the Canaries." Having learnt something about the West Indies, he made several voyages there, carrying with him numbers of negroes to sell, whom he took, partly by the sword, and partly by other means, on the coast of Africa.

Hawkins and the other adventurers who joined him brought home great riches. In the account of those early voyages we see the beginning of a quarrel with Spain, which was to last through the reign of Elizabeth, till Philip sent his great Armada to invade England.

The third and most famous voyage of John Hawkins to the West Indies was called "the troublesome voyage," for it ended in disaster. It was the biggest venture that had yet been made by the English, and Drake took part in it. Hawkins sailed with six ships. There were two "great ships" of the Royal Navy—the *Jesus*, commanded by Hawkins himself, and the *Minion*; the *William and John*, named after and owned by the Hawkins brothers; and three smaller ones, the *Swallow*, the *Angel*, and the *Judith*, the last being under the command of Francis Drake.

They got slaves in Africa and sold them in the West Indies, though not without difficulty, because the Spaniards had been forbidden by their king to trade with the English. As they were about to start on their way home, the ships met with fearful storms, and as the *Jesus* was much shattered, Hawkins made up his mind to seek for haven. They were driven at last into Vera Cruz, the port of the city of Mexico. Here they sheltered, hoping to buy food and repair their fleet. Now in this very port lay treasure which was said to be worth thousands of pounds. It was waiting for the fleet of armed ships which was to take it safely back to Spain. The Spaniards were much dismayed to see the English ships, with their Portuguese ships and prisoners captured on the voyage, come, as they thought, to seize their treasure. It was this very danger they had feared when Hawkins first began his slave trade and disturbed the peace of the Spanish colonies.

Next morning thirteen great ships appeared, and proved to be a Mexican fleet returning with a new Viceroy or Governor from King Philip. A solemn and peaceful agreement was made, and the Spanish ships were moored alongside the English ones, which were already in possession of the harbour. However, the Spaniards afterwards broke faith and fell upon the English, and a great and fierce fight took place, which lasted from ten in the morning until night. The *Angel* and the *Swallow* were sunk, and the *Jesus* so damaged that it could not be brought away.

As the remaining ships were sailing away the Spaniards sent two "fire ships" after them. This was not an unusual way of fighting in those days. The empty, burning ships were sent to try and fire the enemies' ships, and were borne along, flaming, by the wind, an awful and terrifying sight. The men on the *Minion* became panic-stricken, and set sail without orders. Some of the men from the *Judith* followed in a small boat. The rest were forced "to abide the mercy of the Spaniards," which, Hawkins says, he doubts was very little.

"The same night," he goes on, "the *Judith* forsook us in our great misery. In the end, when the wind came larger, we weighed anchor and set sail, seeking for water, of which we had very little. And wandering thus certain days in these unknown seas, hunger forced us to eat hides, cats and dogs, mice, rats, parrots, and monkeys."

Some of the men asked to be put on land, rather than risk shipwreck and starvation in the overcrowded boat. Hawkins did, in the end, get safely home, with his weather-beaten ship, and the survivors of his feeble, starving crew. But he says that, if all the miseries and troubles of this sorrowful voyage were to be written, the tale would be as long as the "Book of Martyrs." Some of the men that were left also reached England, after weary wanderings and years of terrible sufferings. Some were put to death as heretics, and others were sent to the galleys as slaves. Others, more fortunate, were sent to serve in monasteries, where the monks made kind and gentle masters.

Five days before Hawkins reached England, the little *Judith* struggled into Plymouth Harbour with Drake and his load of men. William Hawkins sent him at once to London on horseback, "post, post haste," as the old letters say. He carried letters to the Lords of Council, and to Sir William Cecil, the Chief Secretary of the Queen. So he rode swiftly along the country roads, only stopping to fling himself off one weary, smoking horse on to the back of a fresh one. The people would gather round him as he made the change, and wonder what great news was going to town.

William Hawkins said in his letter: "There is come to Plymouth, at this present hour, one of the small barks

DRAKE CARRYING TO COURT THE NEWS OF HIS VOYAGE.

of my brother's fleet, and as I have neither writing nor anything else from him, I thought it good, and my most bounden duty, to send you the captain of the same bark. He is our kinsman, and is called Francis Drake."

He was to tell the whole story, and the Queen was to hear it. He was to tell of the losses of John Hawkins, and of his absence, which his brother says "is unto me more grief than any other thing in the world."

Drake was much blamed at the time for deserting his general. It is difficult for us to see what he could have done. His little ship was crowded, and he had small store of food and water, and he no doubt thought it best to get home as soon as possible. His story of Spanish treachery and English loss must have roused the country side. The excitement was at its height when the *Minion* appeared off Cornwall.

A man "for goodwill" came riding to William Hawkins, at Plymouth, to get help. He sent a bark, with thirty-four mariners and a store of fresh food and other necessaries. And again letters were sent to London with the news. Haste! Haste! post haste!

Nombre de Dios

It was in January 1569 that the "troublesome voyage" ended for Drake, and in the summer of that year he married a Devonshire girl, named Mary Newman. The stories of his most famous voyages are found in an old book, called "Sir Francis Drake Revived." This was first printed by his descendant, another Sir Francis Drake, in the reign of Charles the First. It was written by some of the voyagers, and it is thought that Drake himself wrote part of it and corrected it. It is supposed that Drake presented the manuscript to Queen Elizabeth, for he dedicates it to her as the "first fruits" of his pen. He also says that his labours by land and sea were not more troublesome than the writing of it.

After his losses and misfortunes in the Indies, it seems that Drake could get no amends from Spain, though he had lost both kinsmen, friends, and goods of some value. Queen Elizabeth could not think of making war with Philip. Her country was poor, her father's navy was ruined. She had no proper army, and she had trouble enough on her hands in France and Scotland.

Therefore Drake decided to help himself in what he was pleased to call his quarrel with the King of Spain. The old writer says that the story of his life shows how "so mean a person righted himself upon so mighty a prince. The one was in his own conceit the mightiest monarch in the world, the other only an English captain."

Drake now made two voyages that really prepared the way for his great and famous one to Nombre de Dios. He probably paid his expenses by plundering ships or selling slaves. On the 24th day of May 1572, Drake started with his ship, the *Pascha* of Plymouth, and the *Swan* of Plymouth, in which his brother, John Drake, was captain. They had on board seventy-three men and boys. All of these came willingly, and had not been *pressed*, or compelled to serve, as the custom then was.

Drake's ships had a very good passage, and never stopped till they reached one of the West Indian Islands, in twenty-five days. Here they stayed three days to refresh the men, and to water the ships. The third day they set sail for the continent. They steered for a bay named formerly by them Port Pheasant. It was a fine, safe harbour. As they rowed ashore in one boat, smoke was seen in the woods. Drake manned and armed the other boats.

When they landed, it was found that a certain Englishman, called John Garret, of Plymouth, had lately been there. Some mariners who had been with Drake in his other voyages had shown him the place.

Garret had left a plate of lead, nailed fast to a mighty, great tree, on which these words were engraved:—

"CAPTAIN DRAKE.

"If you happen to come to this port, make haste away! for the Spaniards which you had with you here, the last year, have betrayed this place, and taken away all you left here. I depart from hence this present day of July, 1572.—

Your very loving friend,
JOHN GARRETS

The smoke came from a fire which Garret and his company had made before they went. It had been burning for at least five days before Drake's arrival. Drake had brought with him "three dainty pinnaces," made in Plymouth, and stored on board ship in pieces. He intended to put them together in this place. So the ships were anchored, and the place simply but strongly fortified with great logs.

Next day an English boat appeared. The captain was James Rance, and he had thirty men, some of whom had been with Drake the year before. They brought with them a Spanish *caravel*, or merchant ship, which they had taken the day before, and a pinnace. They joined Drake's expedition. In seven days the pinnaces' were set up and furnished out of the ships. Some negroes on a neighbouring island told them that the townsfolk of Nombre de Dios were in great fear of the *Cimaroons*, or "Maroons," as our sailors called them. They had attacked the town of Nombre de Dios, and the Governor of Panama was to send soldiers to defend it. These were negroes who had fled some eighty years before from the cruelty of the Spaniards. They had married Indian women, and had grown into a strong fighting tribe, who had two kings of their own, and lived one on the east, and one on the west, of the road from Nombre de Dios to Panama. This was the road by which all the gold and silver from the mines of Peru was sent to the port of Nombre de Dios, to be shipped for Spain. It was carried by trains of mules.

Drake hastened his plans. Three ships and the *caravel* were left with Captain Rance. He chose seventy-three men, for the three pinnaces (the fourth was that taken by Captain Rance), took plenty of arms, and two drums and a trumpet. The men were drilled and given their weapons and arms, which had been kept up till then "very fair and safe in good casks." Drake encouraged them to the attack. In the afternoon they set sail for Nombre de Dios, and were very near before sunset. They lay there under the shore, out of sight of the watch, till dark. Then they rowed near shore as quietly as possible, and waited for the dawn.

But Drake found the men were getting nervous, so when the moon rose "he thought it best to persuade them it was day dawning," and the men had not time to get afraid, for they got there at three in the morning. They landed with no difficulty. But the noise of bells and drums and shouting soon told them that the town was awake and alarmed. Twelve men were left to keep the pinnaces and ensure a safe retreat. Drake's brother, with John Oxenham and sixteen other men, went round behind the King's Treasure-house, and entered the eastern end of the market-place. Drake, with the rest, passed up the broad street into the market-place, with sound of drum and trumpets. They used fire-pikes, or long poles with metal points, to which torches of blazing tow were fastened, and served both to frighten the enemy and to light Drake's men, who could see quite well by them. The terrified townsfolk imagined an army was marching upon them.

After a sharp fight in the market-place the Spaniards fled. Two or three of them were captured, and commanded to show Drake the Governor's house. But he found that only silver was kept there; gold, pearls, and jewels being carried to the King's Treasure-house, not far off.

"This house was very strongly built of lime and stone for safe keeping of the treasure. At the Governor's house we found the great door open where the mules are generally unladen. A candle stood lighted on the top of the stairs, and a fair horse was saddled ready for the Governor himself, or for one of his household. By this light we saw a huge heap of silver in the lower room. It was a pile of bars of silver.

"At this sight our Captain commanded straightly that none of us should touch a bar of silver. We must stand to our weapons, because the town was full of people. There was in the King's Treasure-house, near the waterside, more gold and jewels than all our pinnaces could carry.

This we could presently try to break open, though they thought it so strong.

"But now a report was brought by some of our men that our pinnaces were in danger to be taken, and that we had better get aboard before day. This report was learnt through a negro named Diego, who had begged to be taken on board our ships when we first came. Our Captain sent his brother and John Oxenham to learn the truth. They found the men much frightened, for they saw great troops of armed townsfolk and soldiers running up and down. Presently, too, a mighty shower of rain fell, with a terrible storm of thunder and lightning. It came down violently, as it does in these countries. Before we could reach the shelter at the western end of the King's Treasure-house, some of our bowstrings were wet, and some of our match and powder hurt.

"Our men began to mutter about the forces of the town. But our Captain, hearing, told them: 'He had brought them to the mouth of the treasure of the world; if they went without it, they might blame nobody but themselves afterwards.'

"So soon as the fury of the storm was spent, he gave his men no time to consider their doubts, nor the enemy no time to gather themselves together. He stepped forward and commanded his brother and John Oxenham to break the King's Treasure-house. The rest, with him, were to hold the market-place till the business was done.

"But as he stepped forward his strength and sight

DRAKE WOUNDED AT NOMBRE DE DIOS.

and speech failed him, and he began to faint for loss of blood. And we saw it had flowed in great quantities upon the sand out of a wound in his leg. He had got it in the first encounter, but though he felt some pain he would not make it known till he fainted, and so he frayed it against his will. He saw that some of the men, having already got many good things, would seize any chance to escape further danger. But the blood that filled our very footprints greatly dismayed our company, who could not believe that one man could lose so much blood, and live.

"Even those who were willing to risk more for so good a booty would in no case risk their Captain's life. So they gave him something to drink to recover him, and bound his scarf about his leg to stop the blood. They also entreated him to be content to go aboard with them, there to have his wound searched and dressed, and then to return on shore again if he thought good.

"This they could by no means persuade him to, so they joined force with fair entreaty, and bore him aboard his pinnace. Thus they gave up a rich spoil only to save their Captain's life, being sure that, while they enjoyed his presence and had him to command them, they might recover enough of wealth. But if once they lost him they should hardly be able to get home again. No, nor keep that they had got already. Thus we embarked by break of day, having besides our Captain, many of our men wounded, though none slain but one trumpeter. And though our surgeons were kept busy in providing remedies and salves for their wounds, yet the main care of the Captain was respected by all the rest.

"Before we left the harbour, we took with little trouble the ship of wine for the greater comfort of our company. And though they shot at us from the town we carried our prize to the Isle of Victuals. Here we cured our wounded men, and refreshed ourselves in the goodly gardens which we found there abounding with great store of dainty roots and fruit. There was also great plenty of poultry and other fowls, no less strange than delicate."

Fort Diego

After the return to the ship Captain Rance departed. But Drake had a new plan in his head; he meant to attack Cartagena, the capital of the Spanish Main. Sailing into the harbour in the evening, they found that the townsfolk had been warned that Frenchmen and Englishmen were about. Drake took possession of a large ship that was outward bound. But the townsfolk, hearing of it, took the alarm, rang out their bells, fired their cannon, and got all their soldiers out. Next morning Drake took two more ships near the harbour, one of which was bound to Cartagena with a letter of warning against "Captain Drake." Drake sent his Spanish prisoners on shore, and so ended his first attempt upon Cartagena.

He saw that the coasts were aware of his presence. Yet he did not want to go away till he had discovered the Maroons; for his faithful negro, Diego, had told him that they were friendly to him as the enemy of Spain. This search might take time, and must be done in the smaller boats, which were swifter and could explore the rivers. He had not enough men both to sail the boats and the pinnaces; so he now decided to burn one of the ships and make a store-house of the other. In this way his pinnaces would be properly manned, and he could stay as long as he liked. This was accordingly done. For fifteen days the big ship lay hidden in the Sound of Darien, to make the Spaniards think they had left the coast. Here Drake kept the men busy trimming and cleaning the pinnaces, clearing the ground, and building huts. Diego the negro was a very good builder, and knew the ways of the country well. The men played, too, at bowls and quoits, and shooting with arrows at targets. The smiths had brought forges from England and set them up. Every now and again the pinnaces crept out to sea to plunder passing ships. Much food was put away in different storehouses to serve till they had "made their voyage," as they said, or "made their fortunes," as we should say.

Later, Port Plenty being found an unsafe harbour, they moved to a new place, which they fortified and called Fort Diego. They now prepared to wait five months, because the Maroons had told them that the Spaniards carried no treasure by land during the rainy months. They were not idle during these months, for the ship and fort were left in charge of John Drake, while Captain Drake and John Oxenham went roving in the pinnaces. They had many adventures, being in some peril in their small boats, and always at the mercy of the weather, while at one time they were almost starving. Some of the men got ill with the cold and died, for they had little shelter on board. When they got back to the ships they found all things in good order; but they received the heavy news of the death of

John Drake, the Captain's brother, a young man of great promise.

"Our Captain then resolved to keep close and go no more to sea, but supplied his needs, both for his own company and the Maroons, out of his storehouse. Then ten of our company fell down sick of an unknown disease, and most of them died in a few days. Later, we had thirty men sick at one time. Among the rest, Joseph Drake, another of his brothers, died in our Captain's arms.

"We now heard from the Maroons, who ranged the country up and down for us, to learn what they might for us, that the fleet had arrived from Spain in Nombre de Dios. The Captain prepared to make his journey by land to Panama. He gave Elias Hixon the charge of the ship and company and the Spanish prisoners. Our Captain was advised by the Maroons what provisions to prepare for the long and great journey, what kind of weapons, what store of victuals, and what kind of clothes. He was to take as many shoes as possible, because they had to pass so many rivers with stone and gravel. Twenty-eight of our men had died. A few were left to keep the ship, attend the sick, and guard the prisoners.

"We started on Shrove Tuesday, February the third. At his departure our Captain gave this Master strict charge, in any case not to trust any messenger that should come in his name with any tokens, unless he brought his hand-writing. This he knew could not be copied by the Maroons or the Spaniards."

THE GOLDEN MULE-TRAINS

There were forty-eight men of the party, of whom eighteen only were English. The Maroons carried arms and food, and got more food with their arrows from time to time. Every day they began to march by sunrise, and rested in the heat of the day in shelters made by the Maroons. The third day they came to a little town or village of the Maroons, which was much admired by the sailors for its beauty and cleanliness. "As to their religion," says the story, "they have no kind of priests, only they held the Cross in great awe. But by our Captain's persuasions, they were contented to leave their crosses and to learn the Lord's Prayer, and to be taught something of God's worship."

They begged Drake to stay with them some days, but he had to hasten on. Four of the best guides amongst the Maroons marched on ahead, and broke boughs to show the path to those that followed. All kept strict silence. The way lay through cool and pleasant woods.

"We were much encouraged because we were told there was a great tree about half way, from which we could see at once both the North Sea, from whence we came, and the South Sea, whither we were going.

"The fourth day we came to the height of the desired hill, a very high hill, lying east and west like a ridge between the two seas. It was about ten of the clock. Then Pedro, the chief of the Maroons, took our Captain by the hand, and prayed him to follow him if he wished to see at once two seas, which he had so greatly longed for.

"Here was that goodly and great high tree, in which they had cut and made various steps to get up near the top. Here they had made a convenient bower, where ten or twelve men might easily sit. And here we might, with no difficulty, plainly see the Atlantic Ocean, whence we now came, and the South Atlantic (Pacific) so much desired. South and north of the Tree they had felled certain trees that the prospect might be clearer.

"Our Captain went up to this bower, with the chief Maroon. He had, because of the breeze, as it pleased God, a very fair day. And he saw that sea of which he had heard such golden reports. He prayed Almighty God, of His goodness, to give him life and leave to sail once in an English ship in that sea! Then he called up the rest of our men, and specially he told John Oxenham of his prayer and purpose, if it pleased God to grant him that happiness. He, understanding it, protested that, unless our Captain did beat him from his company, he would follow him, by God's grace! Thus all quite satisfied with a sight of the seas, came down, and after our repast continued our ordinary march through the woods."

The last part of the march was through high pampas

THE MAROON CHIEF SHOWING THE ATLANTIC AND
PACIFIC OCEANS FROM THE TREE-TOP.

grass. But now they began to get glimpses of Panama, and could at last see the ships in the harbour. Now the march had to be more secret and silent than ever, till at length they lay hidden in a grove near the high road from Panama to Nombre de Dios. From here a Maroon was despatched, clothed as a negro of Panama, as a spy. He was to go into the town and learn when the treasure was to be taken from the King's Treasure-house in Panama to Nombre de Dios. This journey to Venta Cruz was always made by night, because of the heat and toil of walking through the pampas grass. But from Venta Cruz to Nombre de Dios they traveled always by day and not by night, because the way lay through fresh, cool woods. The mules were tied together in long trains, and guarded, if possible, by soldiers, for fear of the Maroons.

The spy brought back news in the afternoon that a certain great man intended to go to Spain by the first ship, and was going that night towards Nombre de Dios with his daughter and family. He had fourteen mules, of which eight were laden with gold and one with jewels: There were also two other trains of fifty mules each, mostly laden with food, and with a little silver, which were to come out that night also. Upon hearing this they marched until they came to within two leagues of Venta Cruz. Then Drake lay down with half his men on one side of the way, about fifty paces off, in the long grass. John Oxenham, with the captain of the Maroons and the other half of the men, lay on the other side of the road at the same distance. In about half-an-hour's time they could hear the mules both coming and going from Venta Cruz to Panama, where trade was lively when the fleet was there. The sound of the deep-voiced bells which the mules wore carried far in the still night. The men had been strictly charged not to stir or show themselves, but let all that come from Venta Cruz pass by quietly, for they knew the mules brought nothing but merchandise from there. But one of the men, called Robert Pike, had "drunk too much brandy without water," and forgot himself, and with a Maroon went close to the road.

"And when a cavalier from Venta Cruz, well mounted, with his page running at his stirrup, passed by, he rose up to look, though the Maroon, more cautious, pulled him down and tried to hide him. But by this time the gentleman had noticed that one half of him was white, for we had all put our shirts over our other clothing that we might be sure to know our own men in the pell-mell in the night. The cavalier put spurs to his horse, and rode away at a gallop to warn others.

"The ground was hard and the night was still, and our Captain heard this gentleman's trot change to a gallop. He suspected that we were discovered, but could not imagine by whose fault, nor had he time to search. The gentleman, as we heard afterwards, warned the Treasurer who, fearing Captain Drake had come to look for treasure on land, turned his train of mules aside from the way, and let the others which were coming pass on. Thus, by the recklessness of one of our company, and by the carefulness of that traveler, we were disappointed of a most rich booty. But we thought that God would not let it be taken, for likely it was well gotten by that Treasurer.

"The other two mule trains, which came behind that of the Treasurer, were no sooner come up to us than we stayed and seized on them. One of the chief carriers, a very sensible fellow, told our Captain by what means we were discovered, and counseled us to shift for ourselves betimes, for we should encounter the whole force of the city and country before day would be about us."

Drake and his men were little pleased at the loss of their golden mule-trains, for they had only taken two horse-loads of silver. It was the more provoking that they had been betrayed by one of their own men. There was no help for it, and Drake never "grieved at things past," so they decided to march back the nearest way. Pedro, the chief of the Maroons, said he "would rather die at Drake's foot than leave him to his enemies." When they got near Venta Cruz, they turned back the mules with their drivers. Outside the town the soldiers met them, and a fight took place upon Drake's refusing to surrender.

"The soldiers shot off their whole volley, which, though it lightly wounded our Captain and several of our men, caused death to one only of our company, who was so powdered with hail-shot that we could not recover his life, though he continued all that day afterwards with us. Presently, as our Captain perceived their shot to come slacking, like the last drops of a great shower of rain, he gave his usual signal with his whistle, to answer them with our shot and arrows.

"The Maroons had stepped aside at first for terms of the shot. But seeing that we marched onwards they all rushed forward, one after the other, with their arrows ready in their bows, and their manner of country dance or leap, ever singing, *Yo Pehò! Yo Pehò!* and so got before us. They then continued their leap and song, after the manner of their country wars, till they and we overtook the enemy. Our Maroons, now thoroughly encouraged, when they saw our resolution, broke in through the thickets near the town's end, and forced the enemy to fly. Several of our men were wounded, and one Maroon was run through with one of their pikes, but his courage and mind served him so well that he revenged his own death ere he died, by giving him that deadly wound."

So they entered the town, and stayed there some hours for rest and refreshment, and the Maroons were allowed to carry away some plunder. At sunrise they marched away, for they had been gone from the ship nearly a fortnight, and had left the company weak and sickly. Drake marched cheerfully, and urged on his weary and disappointed men with brave promises, but in the hurried march they had often to go hungry. Three leagues from the port the Maroons had built a camp or village while they were away, and here they persuaded Drake to stop, as it had been built "only for his sake." "And indeed he was the more willing to consent, that our want of shoes might be supplied by the Maroons, who were a great help to us. For all our men complained of the tenderness of their feet, and our Captain himself would join in their complaint, sometimes without cause, but sometimes with cause indeed, which made the rest to bear the burden more easily. These Maroons did us good service all the time they were with us. They were our spies on the journey, our guides, our hunters, and our house wrights, and, had indeed able and strong bodies for carrying our necessities. Yea, many times when some of our company fainted with sickness of weariness, two Maroons would carry him with ease between them, two miles together; and at other times, when need was, they would show themselves no less valiant than industrious, and of good judgment.

"From this town our Captain despatched a Maroon with a token and a certain order to the master. He, all those weeks, kept good watch against the enemy, and shifted in the woods for fresh food, for the relief and recovery of our men left on board."

When the messenger reached the shore he hailed those on the ship, who quickly fetched him on board. He showed Drake's token, the golden toothpick, and gave the message, which was to tell the master to meet him at a certain river. When the master looked at the toothpick, he saw written on it, "By me, Francis Drake." Then be believed the messenger, and prepared what provision he had, and repaired to the mouth of the river. About three o'clock

Drake and his men saw the pinnace, and there was double rejoicing. The wanderers seemed strangely changed in face and plight to those who had lived in rest and plenty on board ship. Drake, indeed, was less so than the others. The fasting and hard marches had done much, but still more "their inward grief, for that they returned without that golden treasure they hoped for, did show her print and footsteps in their faces." But Drake was determined to repeat the attempt.

Home Again

Drake well knew that delay and idleness would soon spoil the spirits of his men, so he at once divided them into two companies, under himself and John Oxenham, to go roving in the two pinnaces in different directions and seek for food and plunder. Some of the Maroons were dismissed with gifts, and the rest remained with a few men on board ship. The Governor of Panama had warned the towns so well that it was useless to attempt them at present. Drake, in the *Minion*, took a frigate of gold and dismissed it, somewhat lighter, to go on its way. John Oxenham, in the *Bear*, took a frigate well laden with food of all kinds. Drake was so pleased with this ship, which was strong and new and shapely, that he kept her as a man-of-war in place of the sunken ship. And the company were heartened with a feast and much good cheer that Easter Day.

Next day the pinnaces met with a French captain out of Newhaven, whose ship was greatly distressed for want of food and water. Drake relieved him, and the captains exchanged gifts and compliments. The French captain sent Drake "a gilt fair scimitar" which had belonged to Henry the Third of France, and had in return a chain of gold and a tablet. This captain brought them the news of the Massacre of St. Bartholomew's Day, and said he thought "those Frenchmen the happiest who were furthest from France, now no longer France but Frenzy." He had heard famous reports of their riches, and wanted to know how he also could "make his voyage." They resolved, after consultation, to take him and twenty of his men to serve for halves. They now sent for the Maroons.

A party was made up of twenty Frenchmen, fifteen Englishmen, and some Maroons. They sailed with a frigate and two pinnaces towards a river called Rio Francisco, to the west of Nombre de Dios. There was not enough water to sail the frigate, so she was left in charge of a mariner to await the return of the pinnaces. They went on, and landed both captains with their force. Those in charge of the pinnaces were ordered to be there the fourth day without fail. The land party went on through the woods towards the high road from Panama to Nombre de Dios, where the mules now went daily. They marched, as before, in silence. They stayed all night a mile from the road, in great stillness, and refreshed themselves. They could hear the carpenters working on their ships, which they did at nights because of the fierce heat of the day. Next morning, the 1st of April, they heard such a number of bells that the Maroons rejoiced exceedingly, and assured them they should now have more gold and silver than they could carry away. And so it came to pass.

For three trains appeared, one of fifty mules and two

of seventy each, and every mule carried 300 lbs. weight of silver, amounting to nearly 30 tons. The leaders of the mules were taken by the heads, and all the rest lay down, as they always do. The fifteen soldiers who guarded each train were routed, but not before they had wounded the French captain sorely, and slain one of the Maroons. They took what silver and gold they could carry, and buried the rest in the burrows made in the earth by the great land crabs under old fallen trees, and in the sand and gravel of a shallow river.

After two hours they marched back through the woods, but had to leave the French captain to rest and recover from his wound. Two of his men willingly stayed with him. Later on a third Frenchman was found to be missing. He had got drunk, and overloaded himself with plunder, and lost himself in the woods. They afterwards found he was taken by the Spaniards in the evening, and, upon. torture, revealed to them where the treasure was hidden.

When they reached the river's mouth, they saw seven Spanish pinnaces at sea, which had come out to search the coasts. This made them fear their own pinnaces were taken. But a storm in the night forced the Spaniards to go home, and also delayed the English pinnaces, for the wind was so contrary and so strong that they could only get half way. For this reason they had fortunately been unseen by the Spaniards.

"But our Captain, seeing their ships, feared lest they had taken our pinnaces, and compelled our men by torture to confess where his ships and frigate were. In this great doubt and perplexity the company feared that all means of returning to their country were cut off, and that their treasure would then serve them to small purpose. But our captain comforted and encouraged us all, saying: 'We should venture no further than he did. It was no time now to fear, but rather to haste to prevent that which was feared. If the enemy have prevailed against our pinnaces (which God forbid!), yet they must have time to search them, time to examine the mariners, time to execute their resolution after it is determined. Before all those times be taken, we may get to our ships, if ye will, though not possibly by land, because of the hills, thickets, and rivers, yet by water. Let us, therefore, make a raft with the trees that are here in readiness, as offering themselves, being brought down to the river happily by this last storm, and let us put ourselves to sea! I will be one, who be the other?'

"John Smith offered himself, and two Frenchmen that could swim very well desired they might accompany our Captain, as did the Maroons likewise. They had prayed our Captain very earnestly to march by land, though it was a sixteen days' journey, in case the ship had been surprised, that he might abide with them always. Pedro was most eager in this, who was fain to be left behind because he could not row.

"The raft was fitted and fast bound; a sail of a biscuit-sack was prepared; an oar was shaped out of a young tree to serve instead of a rudder, to direct their course before the wind.

"At his departure, our Captain comforted the company by promising 'that, if it pleased God he should put his foot in safety on board his frigate, he would, by one means or other, get them all on board, in spite of all the Spaniards in the Indies!'

In this manner pulling off to sea, he sailed some three leagues, sitting up to the waist continually in water, and up to the armpits at every surge of the waves, for the space of six hours upon this raft. And what with the parching of the sun and what with the beating of salt water, they had all of them their skins much fretted away.

"At length God gave them the sight of two pinnaces turning towards them with much wind, but with far greater joy to him than can easily be guessed. So he did cheerfully declare to those three with him, that they were our pinnaces! and that all was safe, so there was no cause of fear!

"But look, the pinnaces not seeing the raft, nor suspecting any such matter, by reason of the wind, and night growing on, were forced to run into a cove behind the point, to take shelter for the night. Our Captain seeing this, and gathering that they would anchor there, put his raft ashore, and ran round the point by land, where he found them. They, upon sight of him, made as much haste as they could to take him and his company on board. For our Captain, on purpose to see what haste they could and would make in extremity, himself ran in great haste, and so made the other three with him, as if they had been chased by the enemy. And so those on board suspected, because they saw so few with him.

"And after his coming on board, when they demanded 'how his company did?' he answered coldly, 'Well!' They all feared that all went scarce well. But he, willing it, rid all doubts, and fill them with joy, took out of his bosom a quoit of gold, thanking God that 'our voyage was made!'"

They then rowed up the river and rescued the others, and brought back such of the treasure as they had been able to carry with them, and all returned to the ships by dawn. There Drake divided the treasure equally by weight between the French and the English. During the next fortnight everything was set in order, and the *Pascha* given to the Spanish prisoners to go home in. Meanwhile a party was sent out to try and rescue the French captain and to seek for the buried treasure. One only of the Frenchmen managed to escape and was saved. Much of the treasure had been discovered by the Spaniards, but not all, and the party returned very cheerful, with thirteen bars of silver and a few quoits of gold. The Frenchmen now left them, having got their shares of the treasure. The ships parted when passing close by Cartagena, which they did in the sight of all the fleets "with a flag of St George on the main top of the frigate, with silk streamers and ancients (national flags) down to the water."

Later on they anchored to trim and rig the frigates and

stow away the provisions, and they tore up and burnt the pinnaces so that the Maroons might have the ironwork. One of the last days Drake desired Pedro and three of the chief Maroons to go through both his frigates and see what they liked. He promised to give them whatever they asked, unless he could not get back to England without it. But Pedro set his heart on the scimitar which the French captain had given to Drake; and knowing Drake liked it no less, he dared not ask for it or praise it. But at last he bribed one of the company to ask for him, with a fine quoit of gold, and promised to give four others to Drake. Drake was sorry, but he wished to please Pedro, who deserved so well, so he gave it to him with many good words. Pedro received it with no little joy, and asked Drake to accept the four pieces of gold, as a token of his thankfulness and a pledge of his faithfulness through life. He received it graciously, but did not keep it for himself but caused it to be cast into the whole adventure, saying that "if he had not been helped to that place he would never have got such a thing, and it was only just that those who shared his burden in setting him to sea should enjoy a share of the benefits."

"Thus with good love and liking, we took our leave of that people. We took many ships during our abode in those parts, yet never burnt nor sunk any, unless they acted as men-of-war against us, or tried to trap us. And of all the men taken in those vessels, we never offered any kind of violence to any, after they were once come into our power.

For we either dismissed them in safety, or kept them with us some longer time. If so, we provided for them as for ourselves, and secured them from the rage of the Maroons against them, till at last, the danger of their discovering where our ships lay being past, for which cause only we kept them prisoners, we set them also free.

"We now intended to sail home the directest and speediest way, and this we happily performed, even beyond our own expectations, and so arrived at Plymouth, on Sunday about sermon-time, August the 9th, 1573.

"And the news of our Captain's return being brought unto his people, did so speedily pass over all the church, and fill their minds with delight and desire to see him, that very few or none remained with the preacher. All hastened to see the evidence of God's love and blessing towards our gracious Queen and country by the fruit of our Captain's labour and success.

TO GOD ALONE BE THE GLORY.

Round the World

So we see that both of Drake's ships, the *Pascha* and the *Swan*, were left behind in the West Indies, and he made a quick voyage home in the well-built Spanish frigate. We hear nothing of Drake for two years after his return to Plymouth. There is a legend that he kept on the seas near Ireland. Elizabeth was still unable and unwilling to go to war with the King of Spain, but she was willing to encourage the sort of warfare that Drake and the other rovers had so successfully carried on against him.

Such companies of adventurers as these that sailed under Drake and Hawkins did a large part of the work of the navy in the time of Elizabeth. The country was saved the expense which private persons were willing to pay to furnish the ships. The Queen herself is known to have shared in the expenses and plunder of some such expeditions, and so she thriftily laid up treasure in England's empty money-chests. But some of her older councillors disliked exceedingly this way of getting rich, and would rather it had been done openly in war, or not at all.

To Drake it seems to have been a very simple affair. He wished, in the first place, as the old book says, "to lick himself whole of the damage he had received from the

Spaniards." So he acted in pirate-fashion to the Spaniards, but not to the French or to the natives of the West Indies. And Drake considered his own cause so just that he never made a secret of his doings. He went at his own risk, for should he be taken by the enemy his country had no power to protect him, as she was not openly at war with Spain. But, on the other hand, he was secretly encouraged, and his gains were immense.

In the second place, Drake wished to attack and injure the Roman Catholic faith whenever and wherever he could. Churchmen had told him that this was a lawful aim. How earnestly he believed it we can see from the story, where he tried to persuade the Maroons to "leave their crosses," which to him were the sign of the hated religion. The terrible tale of the massacre of the Protestants on St. Bartholomew's Day told him by the French captain (who himself fell into the hands of the Spaniards, as we have seen), must have inflamed this feeling in his soul and in those of his men. It made them more eager than ever to fight the enemies of their own faith.

Then, too, the Spaniards founded their rights to own the New World upon a grant from one of the Popes; and the English, now no longer Catholics, denied his power to give it, and claimed the right for themselves to explore and conquer and keep what share they could get.

The King of Spain looked upon Drake as a pirate, but he could not find out how far he had been secretly encouraged by Elizabeth, and Drake was not punished, in spite of Philip's urgent complaints. But he was prevented from sailing away again on a voyage of discovery, though his friends and brothers went, and among them John Oxenham, who was hanged as a pirate by the Spaniards because he had no commission or formal leave from the Queen or the Government to trade in the West Indies.

During this interval Drake took service in Ireland, under the Earl of Essex, furnishing his own ships, "and doing excellent service both by sea and land at the winning of diverse strong forts." The work he took a part in was as harsh and cruel as any that was ever done by fire and sword to make Ireland more desolate. Here he met Thomas Doughty, one of the household of the Earl of Essex, a scholar and a soldier, who became his friend, and sailed with him on his next voyage.

The story of this voyage is told under the name of "The World Encompassed," and in it Drake is said "to have turned up a furrow about the whole world." In 1520 Magellan had discovered the passage south of America from the Atlantic to the Pacific Ocean, since called by his name. Many adventurers had tried to follow him, but all their efforts had ended in disaster, and the Straits had an uncanny name among sailors, and "were counted so terrible in those days that the very thoughts of attempting them were dreadful."

Drake's fleet was made up of five ships—the *Pelican*, which was his flagship, the *Elizabeth*, the *Marigold*, the *Swan*, and the *Christopher*. They took a hundred and sixty

SIR FRANCIS DRAKE.

men and plentiful provisions and stores for the long and dangerous voyage. They also took pinnaces which could be set up when wanted. Nor did Drake forget to "make provision for ornament and delight, carrying to this purpose with him expert musicians, rich furniture (all the vessels for his table, yea, many belonging to the cook-room, being of pure silver)."

They started on November 15, 1577, but were forced by a gale to put back into Plymouth for repairs, and started out again on December 13. The sailors were not told the real aim of the voyage, which was to "sail upon those seas greatly longed for." They were too full of fears and fancies. The unknown was haunted in their minds with devils and hurtful spirits, and in those days people still believed in magic.

They picked up several prizes on their way out, notably a large Portuguese ship, whose cargo of wine and food was valuable to the English ships. Drake sent the passengers and crew on shore, but kept the pilot, Numa da Silva; who gives one account of the voyage, and was most useful, as he knew the coasts so well. One of Drake's main cares on this voyage, we are told, was to keep the fleet together as much as possible, to get fresh water, and to refresh the men, "wearied with long toils at sea," as often as possible. He decided to lessen the number of the ships, for "fewer ships keep better company," and he looked for a harbour to anchor in.

"Our General," says the book, "especially in matters

of moment, was never one to rely only on other men's care, how trusty or skilful soever they might seem to be. But always scorning danger, and refusing no toil, he was wont himself to be one, whosoever was a second, at every turn, where courage, skill, or industry was to be employed. Neither would he at any time entrust the discovery of these dangers to another's pains, but rather to his own experience in searching out and sounding of them."

So in this case Drake himself went out in the boat and rowed into the bay. The *Swan*, the *Christopher*, and the prize were sacrificed, their stores being used for the other ships.

On the 20th of June they anchored in a very good harbour, called by Magellan Fort St. Julian. Here a gibbet stood upon the land, and in this place Magellan is supposed to have executed some disobedient and rebellious men of his company. In this port Drake began to "inquire diligently into the actions of Master Thomas Doughty, and found them not to be such as he looked for."

(Doughty is said to have plotted to kill Drake or desert him, and take his place as commander, or at any rate to force him to go back, to the ruin of the voyage.)

Whereupon the company was called together, and the particulars of the cause made known to them, which were found partly by Master Doughty's own confession, and partly by the evidence of the fact, to be true. Which when our General saw, although his private affection to Master Doughty (as he then in the presence of us all sacredly protested) was great; yet the care he had of the state of the voyage, of the expectation of her Majesty, and of the honour of his country, did more touch him (as indeed it ought) than the private respect of one man. So that the cause being thoroughly heard, and all things done in good order, as near as might be to the course of our laws in England, it was concluded that Master Doughty, should receive punishment according to the quality of the offence. And he, seeing no remedy but patience for himself, desired before his death to receive the Communion, which he did, at the hands of our minister, and our General himself accompanied him in that holy action...

"And after this holy repast, they dined also at the same table together, as cheerfully, in sobriety, as ever in their lives they had done aforetime, each cheering up the other, and taking their leave, by drinking each to other, as if some journey only had been in hand.

"And the place of execution being ready, he having embraced our General, and taken his leave of all the company, with prayer for the Queen's Majesty and our realm, in quiet sort laid his head to the block, where he ended his life. This being done, our General made various speeches to the whole company, persuading us to unity, obedience, love and regard of our voyage. And to help us to this, he willed every man the next Sunday following to prepare himself to receive the Communion as Christian brethren and friends ought to do, which was done in very reverent sort, and so with good contentment every man went about his business."

On the 11th of August, as quarrelling still continued, Drake ordered the whole ships' companies ashore. They all went into a large tent, and the minister offered to make a sermon. "Nay, soft, Master Fletcher," said Drake, "I must preach this day myself; although I have small skill in preaching.... I am a very bad speaker, for my bringing up hath not been in learning."

He then told them that for what he was going to say he would answer in England and before her Majesty. He and his men were far away from their country and friends, and discords and mutiny had grown up among them. "By the life of God," said Drake, "it doth take my wits from me to think on it. Here is such quarrels between the sailors and the gentlemen as it doth make me mad to hear it. But, my masters, I must have it left [off], for I must have the gentleman to haul and draw with the mariner, and the mariner with the gentleman. What, let us show ourselves all to be of a company, and let us not give occasion to the enemy to rejoice at our decay and overthrow. I would know him that would refuse to set his hand to a rope, but I know there is not any such here...."

He then offered to send any home that liked in the *Marigold*, a well-furnished ship "but let them take heed that they go homeward, for if I find them in my way I will surely sink them, therefore you shall have time to consider here until to-morrow; for by my troth I must needs be plain with you now."

"Yet the voice was that none would return, they would all take such part as he did." And so, after more of such "preaching," they were told to forget the past, and "wishing all men to be friends, he willed them to depart about their business."

Round the World (Continued)

On the 20th of August the three ships entered the Straits of Magellan. Before the "high and steep grey cliffs, full of black stars," of Cape Virgins, at the entrance against which the beating seas looked like whales spouting, the fleet did homage to the Queen. The name of the *Pelican* also was changed to the *Golden Hind* in remembrance of Drake's "friend and favourer, Sir Christopher Hatton, whose crest was a golden hind. In sixteen days they reached the "South Sea," Drake himself having rowed on ahead of the fleet with some of his gentlemen to find out the passage. He had meant to land, and leave "a monument of her Majesty graven in metal," which he had brought with him for that purpose, but there was no anchoring, as the wind did not let them stay; for a fearful storm arose and separated the ships, and threatened to send them all to the bottom of the sea. The *Marigold*, indeed, went down with all hands and the *Elizabeth*, "partly by the negligence of those that had charge of her, partly through a kind of desire that some in her had to be out of all those troubles and to be at home again, returned back the same way by which they came forward, and so coasting Brazil, they arrived in England on June 2nd the year following." So that now, as the story quaintly says, the other ship, if she had been still called the *Pelican*, would indeed have been a pelican alone in the wilderness. Never did they think there had been such a storm "since Noah's Flood," for it lasted fifty-two days. The ship was driven south of the continent of America. At this time it was generally believed that another great continent stretched to the south of the Straits, which was called the unknown land, "wherein many strange monsters lived." And now, when Drake had discovered this idea to be false, their troubles ended for the time, the storm ceased, but they were in great grief for the loss of their friends, and still hoped to meet the missing ships again.

They sailed northwards of America till they landed on an island to get water. Here they were treacherously attacked by Indians, who took them to be the hated Spaniards. The nine persons who were in the boat were all wounded, and Drake's faithful servant, Diego the negro, died of his wounds, and one other. Drake himself was shot in the face under the right eye, and badly wounded in the head. They were in the worst case, because the chief doctor was dead, and the other in the *Elizabeth*. There was none left them but a boy, "whose goodwill was more than any skill he had." But owing to Drake's advice, and "the putting to of every man's help," all were cured in the end.

They sailed on, and having picked up a friendly Indian who served as a pilot, they reached the harbour of Valparaiso. A ship which was lying in the harbor was seized, and then the town and the Spaniards discovered that Drake had reached the shores of the Pacific. On the coast the ship was trimmed and the pinnace put together, in which Drake himself set out to search the creeks and inlets where the ship could not sail. Grief for the absence of their friends still remained with them. Still searching for the lost ships, they sailed northwards on to Lima, where they got the news that a great Spanish ship had sailed from there a fortnight before, laden with treasure. Drake at once gave chase, hoping to take her before she reached Panama. The first man who sighted her was promised a chain of gold. The ship was overtaken and captured off Cape San Francisco. She was "the great glory of the South Sea," and laden with gold, silver, plate, and jewels, all of which the English took. After six days the Spanish ship was dismissed, "somewhat lighter than before," to Panama. To the master of the ship, Saint Juan de Anton, he gave a letter to protect him if he fell in with the missing English ships.

"Master Winter," it says, "if it pleaseth God that you should chance to meet with this ship of Saint Juan de Anton, I pray you use him well, according to my word and promise given unto them. And if you want anything that is in this ship of Saint Juan de Anton, I pray you pay them double the value for it, which I will satisfy again, and command your men not to do any hurt; desiring you, for the Passion of Christ, if you fall into any danger, that you will not despair of God's mercy, for He will defend you from all danger, and bring us to our desired haven, to whom be all honour, glory, and praise for ever and ever. Amen.—Your sorrowful Captain, whose heart is heavy for you.—FRANCIS DRAKE

The next prizes captured yielded treasure of a different kind, though equally precious. These were some charts with sailing directions, taken from two Chinese pilots. The owner of the next large Spanish ship captured by Drake has left an interesting account of him.

He says that "the English General is the same who took Nombre de Dios five years ago. He is a cousin of John Hawkins, and his name is Francis Drake. He is about thirty-five years of age, of small size, with a reddish beard, and is one of the greatest sailors that exist, both from this skill and his power of commanding. His ship is of near four hundred tons, sails well, and has a hundred men all in the prime of life, and as well trained for war as if they had been old soldiers of Italy. Each one is specially careful to keep his arms clean. He treats them with affection and they him with respect. He has with him nine or ten gentlemen, younger sons of the leading men in England, who form his council. He calls them together on every occasion and hears what they have to say, but he is not bound by their advice, though he may be guided by it. He has no privacy; those of whom I speak all dine at his table, as well as a Portuguese pilot whom he has brought from England, but who never spoke a word while I was on board. The service is of silver, richly gilt, and engraved with his arms. He has, too, all possible luxuries, even to perfumes, many of which he told me were given him by the Queen. None of these gentlemen sits down or puts on his hat in his presence without repeated permission. He dines and sups to the music of violins. His ship carries thirty large guns and a great quantity of ammunition, as well as craftsmen who can do necessary repairs. He has two artists who portray the coast in his own colours, a thing which troubled me much to see, because everything is put so naturally that any one following him will have no difficulty."

Drake wished to find his way home by the north of America into the Atlantic. Out in this he was not successful, for the weather was very severe, and tried the men too much; meanwhile, they found a convenient haven in a little bay above the harbour of San Francisco, and now known as "Drake's Bay." Here they stayed a month, repairing a leak in the ship and refreshing the men. They then set sail, and saw nothing but air and sea for sixty-eight days, till they reached some islands. These they named the "Islands of Thieves," on account of the behaviour of the natives. In November they came to the islands of the Moluccas, where Drake had a splendid reception.

They then sailed on till they arrived at a little island, which they called the "Island of Crabs." Here they pitched their tents, and set up forges to repair the ironwork of the ship and the iron-hooped casks. Those that were sickly soon grew well and strong in this happy island.

On the 9th of January the ship ran aground on a dangerous shoal, and struck twice on it; "knocking twice at the door of death, which no doubt had opened the third time."

Nothing but instant death was expected, and the whole ship's company fell to praying. As soon as the prayers were said, Drake spoke to the men, telling them how they must think of their souls, and speaking of the joys of heaven "with comfortable speeches." But he also encouraged them to bestir themselves, and he himself set the example, and got the pumps to work, and freed the ship of water. The ship was fast upon "hard and pinching rocks, and did tell us plain she expected continually her speedy despatch as soon as the sea and winds should come... so that if we stay with her we must perish with her." The other plan, of leaving her for the pinnace, seemed to them "worse than a thousand deaths."

After taking the Communion and listening to a sermon, they eased the ship by casting goods into the sea—"three ton of cloves, eight big guns, and certain meal and beans"; making, as an old writer says, a kind of gruel of the sea round about. After they had been in this state from eight o'clock at night till four o'clock next afternoon, all in a moment the wind changed, and "the happy gale drove them off the rocks again, and made of them glad men."

The rest of the homeward voyage was less adventurous, and on the 18th of June they passed the Cape of Good

Hope, "a most stately thing, and the fairest cape we saw in the whole circumference of the earth."

On the 26th of September they "safely, and with joyful minds and thankful hearts, arrived at Plymouth, having been away three years."

Sir Francis

It was in the autumn of 1580 that Drake returned from his three years' voyage. Winter had brought the news home that Drake had entered the Straits of Magellan, but since then only vague rumours of his death at the hands of the Spaniards had reached England. Had he met such a fate, Sir William Cecil (now Lord Burghley) and his party at Court would not have been sorry; for they disliked piracy, and wished to avoid a war with Spain.

This was more to be dreaded than ever, as at the death of the King of Portugal, Philip had seized his crown and vast possessions, and was now the most powerful prince in Europe, since he owned the splendid Portuguese fleet. Hitherto, Philip had only warships for the protection of his treasure-ships, and they could not be spared. He was now known to be preparing, in his slow way, a great Armada.

But Drake had not been hanged for a pirate, and this the Spaniards knew very well. They clamoured for the restoration of his plunder, or the forfeit of his life. At this time an army of Italian and Spanish soldiers, under the command of a famous Spanish officer, had been landed in Ireland to help the Catholic Irish in their rebellion against Queen Elizabeth. These soldiers were said to have been sent by the orders of the Pope. Finding the prospects of success too poor, the Spanish officer withdrew his men, and they escaped by sea; but the Italian soldiers, who numbered 600, were overpowered by the English, and all except a few officers, who could pay a ransom, were slaughtered in cold blood. Thus Philip's attempt to strike a secret blow in Elizabeth's fashion was met by her with cruelty as relentless as his own; but Elizabeth made this attempt an excuse for refusing to make an inquiry into Drake's doings in the West.

"The news of his home-coming in England was," we are told, "by this his strange wealth, so far-fetched, marvellous strange, and of all men held impossible and incredible. But both proving true, it fortuned that many misliked it and reproached him. Besides all this there were others that devised and divulged" (made up and spread about) "all possible disgraces" (base charges) "against Drake and his followers, terming him the Master Thief of the Unknown World. Yet nevertheless the people generally with exceeding admiration applauded his wonderful long adventures and rich prize."

Drake at once sent a message to tell the Queen of his return. He was told he had nothing to fear, and was summoned to Court. He took with him some horseloads of gold and silver and jewels. The Queen treated him with great favour, and refused to take the advice of Burghley and others, who wished to send the treasure back to Spain. Unlike them, she took her share of the profits, and also the fine gifts Drake had brought for her. "But it grieved him not a little," we are told, "that some prime courtiers refused the gold he offered them, as gotten by piracy." He and his men had made golden fortunes.

The Spanish Ambassador naturally "burned with passion" against Drake, and considered his presence at Court an insult to his king. "For he passes much time with the Queen," he wrote to Philip, "by whom he is highly favoured."

It was an insult Philip still felt himself unable to avenge. Elizabeth had made a fresh treaty with France, and Philip's best generals knew the difficulties of an attack on England thus strengthened. Besides, the Dutch, whom Elizabeth was helping, were his desperate enemies; for they were fighting for faith and country and freedom, and to do this makes bold soldiers. So Philip the prudent had to content himself with making plans for his great Armada.

Meantime Drake sunned himself in the Court favour, and books and pictures and songs were made in his praise.

The *Golden Hind* was brought ashore at Deptford, and became a resort for sightseers. But in spite of much patching she became so old that she had to be broken up, and the last of her timbers were made into a chair, which is still kept in a quiet Oxford library. So the ship ends her days far away from the sound of the sea, and of the gay throngs that used to make merry and dance on her decks.

On the 4th of April the Queen paid a State visit to the ship, and ordered that it should be preserved for ever.

QUEEN ELIZABETH KNIGHTING DRAKE ON BOARD
THE *GOLDEN HIND* AT DEPTFORD.

A fine banquet was served on board, and there, before the eyes of hundreds of onlookers, Elizabeth knighted the "pirate captain." She said jestingly that the King of Spain had demanded Drake's head, and now she had a gold sword to cut it off. Thus Elizabeth openly defied the Spaniards, who were still raging over their stolen treasure.

But there were some not in Spain who also thirsted for revenge upon Drake. Thomas Doughty's young brother was his unforgiving foe. The case was never brought to Court or indeed to light; but young Doughty wrote a letter in which he said "that when the Queen did knight Drake she did then knight the greatest knave, the vilest villain, the foulest thief, and the cruelest murderer that ever was born." The Spaniards bribed him to try and murder Drake. We hear that he was put in prison, and we never hear of his release.

In 1581 Drake was made Mayor of Plymouth. In 1583 his wife died. He was then a member of Parliament. Two years later he married Mary Sydenham. He never had any children.

The Queen now appointed Drake among others to inquire into the state of the navy; he was to see to the repairing of ships, to the building of new ones, and to the means of furnishing them with stores in case of sudden war. From this time onwards the thought of a Spanish invasion was a constant fear in the minds of the English people. But Philip was unready, and Elizabeth unwilling to be the first to begin a war. Elizabeth changed her mind and her plans in a way that must have been maddening to the men who did her work. One good result of her indecision was that England was better prepared for the invasion. In those long years of private warfare money had been gathering, and the navy made strong and ready for work. But for men of action, who like to make a plan and stick to it, and go through with it at all costs, Elizabeth's delays and recalls were bewildering and unreasonable.

In 1585 Philip seized a fleet of English corn-ships trading in his own ports. Then, at last, Drake's long-talked-of expedition against the Spanish settlements was got ready and sent out. He had about thirty ships, commanded by some of the most famous captains of the time, men like Fenner, Frobisher, and Wynter, who afterwards fought against the Armada. His general of the soldiers was Christopher Carleill, "a man of long experience in wars both by sea and land," and who was afterwards said to direct the service "most like a wise commander." Drake's ship was the *Elizabeth Bonaventure*.

After a week spent in capturing ships, the fleet anchored at the Bayona Islands, off Vigo Bay. The Governor of Bayona was forced to make terms. He sent "some refreshing, as bread, wine, oil, apples, grapes, and marmalade, and such like." The people, filled with terror, were seen to remove their possessions into boats to go up the Vigo River, inland, for safety. Many of these were seized; most of them were loaded only with household stuff, but one contained the "church stuff of the high church of Vigo, a great cross of silver of very fair embossed work and double-gilt all over, having cost them a great mass of money."

The fleet now went on its way by the Canary Islands. When Santiago was reached, Carleill landed with a thousand troops and took possession of the fortress and the town, for both had been forsaken. Here they planted the great flag, "which had nothing on it but the plain English cross; and it was placed towards the sea, that our fleet might see St. George's Cross flourish in the enemy's fortress." Guns were found ready loaded in various places about the town, and orders were given that these should be shot off "in honour of the Queen's Majesty's Coronation day, being the 17th of November, after the yearly custom in England. These were so answered again by the guns out of all the ships in the fleet, as it was strange to hear such a thundering noise last so long together." No treasure was taken at Santiago, but there was food and wine. The town was given to the flames in revenge for wrongs done to old William Hawkins of Plymouth some years before.

They had not been many days at sea before a mortal sickness suddenly broke out among the men. They anchored off some islands, where the Indians treated them very kindly, carried fresh water to the ships, and gave them food and tobacco. The tobacco was a welcome gift, to be used against the infection of the mysterious sickness which was killing the men by hundreds. They passed Christmas on an island to refresh the sick and cleanse and air the ships.

Then Drake resolved, with the consent of his council, to attack the city of St. Domingo, while his forces were "in their best strength." This was the oldest and most important city in the Indies, and was famous for its beauty and strength. It had never been attempted before, although it was so rich, because it was strongly fortified.

Some boats were sent on in advance of the fleet. They learned from a pilot, whose boat they captured, that the Castle of St. Domingo was well armed, and that it was almost impossible to land on the dangerous coast; but he showed them a possible point ten miles from the harbour. In some way Drake had sent messages to the Maroons, who lived on the hills behind the town. At midnight, on New Year's Day, the soldiers were landed, Drake himself steering a boat through the surf. The Maroons met them, having killed the Spanish watchman.

"Our General, having seen us all landed in safety to the west of that brave city of St. Domingo, returned to his fleet, bequeathing us to God and the good conduct of Master Carleill, our Lieutenant-General."

The troops divided and met in the market-place; and as those in the castle were preparing to meet Drake's attack from the sea, they were surprised from behind by the soldiers marching upon them with flags flying and music playing. The fleet ceased firing while the fate of the town was decided in a battle. By night Drake was in possession of the castle, the harbour, and shipping. One of the ships captured they named the *New Year's Gift*.

But after all there was little of the fabled treasure to be found. The labour in the gold and silver mines had killed the native Indians, and the mines were no longer worked. There was plenty of food and wine to be had, woollen and linen cloth and silk. But there was little silver; the rich people used dishes of china and cups of glass, and their beautiful furniture was useless as plunder. The town had to pay a large sum of money for its ransom, and the English stayed a month, and fed at its expense, and took away with them guns and merchandise and food and numbers of galley-slaves, whom they set free.

Cartagena, the capital of the Spanish Main, was the last town to be taken, and it had been warned. It had natural defences, which made it very difficult to attack. Drake, as we know, had been there before, and often, since then, he must have dreamed of taking it. He triumphantly steered his fleet by a very difficult channel into the outer harbour. He then threatened the fort with his guns while the soldiers were secretly landed by night. They made their way to the town by the shore, "wading in the sea-wash," and so avoiding the poisoned stakes which had been placed in the ground in readiness for them. They also routed a company of horse soldiers sent out from the fort, as the place where they met was so "woody and scrubby" as to be unfit for horses. So they pushed on till they made a "furious entry" into the town, nor paused till the market-place was won, and the people fled into the country, where they had already sent their wives and children.

A large price or ransom was paid for this town, equal, it is said, to a quarter of a million of our money; but it was far less than Drake had at first demanded. But "the inconvenience of continual death" forced them to go, for the sickness was still taking its prey from among the men, and it also forced them to give up an attempt upon Nombre de Dios and Panama.

The voyage had been disappointing in the matter of plunder. Most of the treasure had been taken away from the towns before the English came, and many of the officers had died.

They considered the idea of remaining in Cartagena and sending home for more troops. They would have had a fine position; but they decided that their strength was not enough to hold the town and also man the fleet against a possible attack by the Spaniards from the sea. So the lesser ransom was accepted; the officers offering to give up their shares to the "poor men, both soldiers and sailors, who had adventured their lives against the great enemy." They then returned to England, only stopping to water the ships. They landed again at St. Augustine, on the coast of Florida, where they destroyed a fort and took away the guns and a pay-chest containing two thousand pounds.

"And so, God be thanked, we in good safety arrived at

Portsmouth the 28th of July 1586, to the great glory of God, and to no small honour to our Prince, our Country, and Ourselves."

Cadiz

When Drake returned to England, it was to hear the news of the "Babington plot." This was a plot to assassinate Elizabeth, and to place Mary of Scotland on the throne. In 1587 Mary was beheaded. In Philip's eyes the time had at last become ripe for an invasion of England. Now that Mary was dead, there was less danger of France and Scotland joining forces. And Philip, as a descendant of John of Gaunt, could put in a claim that the throne of England, at the death of Elizabeth, should come to himself or his daughter.

The Armada was getting ready to sail in the summer. In April, however, Drake was sent out again with a small fleet. His flag-ship was again the *Elizabeth Bonaventure*. His second in command was William Borough.

His orders were "to prevent the joining together of the King of Spain's fleet out of their different ports. To keep victuals from them. To follow them in case they should come out towards England or Ireland. To cut off as many of them as he could, and prevent their landing. To set upon the West Indian ships as they came or went."

But no sooner was he instructed than the Queen changed her bold orders to milder ones. He was not to enter any port by force, nor to offer violence to any towns, or ships in harbour. But Drake had got away to sea without the second orders, and acted on the first.

He had heard that the ships were gathering in Cadiz harbour, and there he decided boldly to seek for them. The outer and inner harbours of Cadiz were crowded with shipping, most of which was getting ready for the invasion of England. Drake's fleet sailed in, routed the defending galleys, and made havoc among the ships, about thirty-seven of which were captured, burnt, or sunk. One was a large ship belonging to the Marquis of Santa Cruz. They carried away four ships laden with wine, oil, biscuits, and dried fruit; "departing thence," as Drake says, "at our pleasure, with as much honour as we could wish." They were chased by Spanish galleys, which did little harm, for the wind favoured the English as they sailed away from Cadiz.

The Spaniards thought Drake had gone to stop the treasure fleet. But Drake wished to stop the Armada, which was a much greater affair. He knew now that Santa Cruz was making his headquarters at Lisbon. Ships were gathering in the north of Spain. Recalde, one of the best Spanish commanders, was waiting with a small fleet off Cape St. Vincent, to protect the treasure fleet when it arrived. Fifteen big ships had escaped the attack in Cadiz harbour. The ships were to meet in Lisbon, where Santa Cruz was collecting stores and food.

Recalde succeeded in escaping Drake, and took his

ships safely into Lisbon. Drake resolved to secure the station he had left. This was the castle of Sagres, near Cape St. Vincent. His own officers were staggered with the boldness of his plan, and Borough solemnly protested. He had urged caution before Cadiz harbour; again he pleaded for a council of war. He was of an older school of seamen than Drake, and was horrified at the ways of the man who was born, as it has been said, "to break rules."

Drake was most indignant at his action, and put him under arrest, while Borough expected daily that "the Admiral would have executed upon me his bloodthirsty desire, as he did upon Doughty."

After reading the accounts of Drake in the stories of the different voyages, we can understand how his men adored his spirit, and flocked to his ship to serve under his flag. To them there was something magical, and to the Spaniards, something uncanny, in his luck. The English called him "Fortune's child," and the Spanish called him "the Devil." But some of the officers who served with him must have liked him less. He made his plans swiftly, and generally well; but the doing of them had to be swift and sure. Like many great men he knew he was right, but could not stop to reason or argue about his course. He acted upon the instinct of his genius, with a sure and shining faith in himself, which must have been hateful to smaller men. In the days of his later voyages, when he had not the undivided control of his expedition, he failed,

DRAKE AT THE TAKING OF SAGRES CASTLE.

as he never did when he was alone, "with the ships not pestered with soldiers," as he once said.

The taking of the castle of Sagres seemed almost an impossibility, so well did the rocks and steep cliffs defend the fort. Drake himself commanded the attack on land, and in the end helped to carry and pile the faggots against the castle gate. The commander was slain, and then the fort surrendered. Thus Drake took possession of one of the best places on the coast of Spain for ships to anchor and get water.

Meanwhile, the rest of the fleet had taken and burnt fifty ships laden with wood and hoops of seasoned wood, for which Santa Cruz was waiting to make his water-casks. The loss of these did much damage to the Armada, and helped to ruin it.

On the 20th of May, having disarmed the fort of Sagres by throwing the big guns over the cliffs into the sea, Drake brought his fleet to anchor is Cascaes Bay, south of Lisbon. He seems to have judged Lisbon too strong to attack from the sea. He was prepared to "distress the ships" had they come out; and he offered battle to Santa Cruz, who, however, was short of powder and shot, and had no ships ready as yet for action.

So Drake went back to Sagres to clean his ships and refresh his men. He then sailed for the Azores. A storm parted the ships, and on the few that were left the men were anxious to go home. The ship on which Borough was still a prisoner, deserted. Drake believed that Borough was responsible for this; and, though he was beyond reach, in his anger Drake sentenced him, with his chief officers, to death as mutineers.

Drake went on with his nine remaining ships, and came upon a splendid prize, the big *San Felipe*, the greatest ship in all Portugal, richly laden with spice, china, silk, and chests of gold and jewels. This prize was valued at nearly a million pounds; and, besides, she carried secret papers of great value concerning the East India trade.

On the 26th of June, Drake returned home after his brilliant campaign. Santa Cruz had indeed gone out to chase him, but it was too late.

Borough was not found guilty by the court of law where Drake accused him; but his grief of mind endured long. Some time after, he wrote that "he was very fain to ease it as he might, hoping in good time he should."

The Great Armada

Drake's raid upon the Spanish coast made it impossible for the Armada to sail in 1587. But after waiting so long Philip made his preparations with an almost feverish haste. The death of his great general, Santa Cruz, hindered his plans very much. Santa Cruz was a commander of experience and renown, and the man most fitted, both by his rank and his qualities, to undertake "the enterprise of England."

The man chosen to succeed him was the Duke of Medina Sidonia, whose exalted rank seems to have been his chief claim to the difficult place into which he was thrust by Philip. He had no desire to take the place; he wrote to Philip and told him quite simply that he was no seaman, and knew little about naval fighting and less about England. But he was ordered to take the fleet into the English Channel and take possession of Margate. He was then to send ships to bring the Duke of Parma and his army in safety to England, when Parma was to assume the command of the expedition.

But, after all, the Armada was not ready to sail till July 1588, and the months between January and then were filled by the English with preparations for defence. They had to face the difficulties, much greater then than now, of keeping both men and ships on the seas, and yet fit for action. Life on board ship tried the men very severely. We have seen how often sickness broke out among the sailors if they were kept long to their crowded, unhealthy quarters. The feeding of both navies seems to have been a task of great difficulty. This was due to the hurried demand for vast quantities of stores, such as biscuit and salt meat. The Spaniards, too, owing to Drake's foresight, had lost their water-casks, and had to depend on new ones of unseasoned wood, which leaked.

Lord Howard, a cousin of the Queen, was made Lord High Admiral of England, and Drake was his Vice Admiral and John Hawkins his Rear-Admiral. With them served many other famous men, such as Fenner, Frobisher, Wynter, and Seymour, and many younger men from noble families. All were working hard, with spirits stretched to an unusual pitch of endurance. In the letters they wrote about the business in hand to the Queen and her Ministers of State there is a note of high courage and defiance; and a distant echo comes down to us from the dim old letters of all the stir and bustle as the men gathered to the ships, and of the hum of excitement about the clamouring dockyards. The shipwrights were working day and night. Lord Howard says he has been on board every ship "where any man may creep," and thanks God for their good state, and that "never a one of them knows what a leak means." Sir William Wynter tells how badly the ships had suffered in the winter storms, but adds: "Our ships doth show themselves like gallants here. I assure you it will do a man's heart good to behold them; and would to God the Prince of Parma were upon the seas with all his forces, and we in the view of them; then I doubt not but that you should hear we would make his enterprises very unpleasant to him."

The ships are always spoken of like live creatures, and their personal histories are well known and remembered. Lord Howard says of his Ark (which was bought of Sir Walter Raleigh by the Queen): "And I pray you tell her Majesty from me that her money was well given for the Ark *Raleigh*, for I think her the odd (only) ship in the world for all conditions; and truly I think there can no great ship make me change and go out of her." And again: "I mean not to change out of her I am in for any ship that ever was made."

Drake had "her Majesty's very good ship the *Revenge*," which was so famous then and afterwards. Lord Henry Seymour writes from on board "the *Elizabeth Bonaventure*, the fortunate ship where Sir Francis Drake received all his good haps." Howard and Drake, with other commanders of experience, were of one mind; they wanted to go out and meet the enemy upon the coasts of Spain, and so prevent the Spanish fleet from ever reaching England.

Howard pressed this opinion as that of men whom the world judged to be the wisest in the kingdom. But the

Queen was unwilling to send the fleet away, and she still talked of making peace.

Both the Spaniards and the English were persuaded that God was fighting with them. Philip told the Duke of Medina Sidona, that as the cause was the cause of God, he could not fail. In England Drake was saying that "the Lord is on our side"; and Fenner wrote to the Queen: "God mightily defend my gracious Mistress from the raging enemy; not doubting that all the world shall know and see that her Majesty's little army, guided by the finger of God, shall beat down the pride of His enemies and hers, to His great glory." Nowadays we do not look upon our enemies as necessarily the enemies of God.

Howard's letters show a very noble mind. He grudged no time or labour in the ordering of his fleet, down to the smallest matters. He is full of care for the mariners, and is anxious that they should be well paid and fed. He takes the advice of Drake and the other seamen of greater experience than himself.

The fleet did at last go out, but was driven back by the winds; and suddenly, after the fret and worry and strain of all those months, there is a pause, and Howard writes: "Sir, I will not trouble you with any long letter; we are at this present otherwise occupied than with writing. Upon Friday, at Plymouth, I received intelligence that there was a great number of ships descried off the Lizard: whereupon, although the wind was very scant, we first warped out of harbour that night, and upon Saturday turned out very hardly, the wind being at southwest; and about three of the clock in the afternoon, descried the Spanish fleet, and did what we could to work for the wind, which by this morning we had recovered... At nine of the clock we gave them fight, which continued until one.... Sir, the captains in her Majesty's ships have behaved themselves most bravely and like men hitherto, and I doubt not will continue, to their great commendation... Sir, the southerly wind that brought us back from the coast of Spain brought them out."

William Hawkins, then Mayor of Plymouth, writes that the "Spanish fleet was in view of this town yesternight, and the Lord Admiral passed to the sea and out of sight." They could see the fleets fighting, the English being to windward of the enemy. He was sending out men as fast as he could find ships to carry them.

There is a legend that Drake and his officers were playing bowls on Plymouth Hoe when the news that the Armada was in the Channel was brought to him by the captain of a pinnace. Drake calmly finished his game, the story says, saying there was time to do that and to beat the Spaniards too.

As the Spanish ships lay in the English Channel, blinded with the mist and rain, the Duke sent a boat to get news. Four fishermen of Falmouth were brought away who had that evening seen the English fleet go out of Plymouth, "under the charge of the English Admiral and of Drake."

The Spaniards had come out ready to fight in the old

DRAKE AT BOWLS ON PLYMOUTH HOE.

way, in which they had won so many brilliant victories. They had always fought their naval battles with great armies on great ships, much as they would fight on land. The soldiers despised big guns, and liked better the bravery of a close fight, "with hand-thrusts and push of pike." The sailors were not prepared to fight at all, but with the help of slaves they sailed the big galleys and fighting ships, and the swarm of smaller troop-ships and store-ships that swelled the numbers of the fleet which carried an army.

The numbers of the ships on both sides are now said to have been not so very unequal. If the Spaniards could have fought in their own way, they must have been easily victorious. But the English had got the wind at their back and the enemy in front of them, and being better masters of their ships, they had the choice, and they chose to fight at a distance, and never to board the big ships till they were already helpless.

Their ships were newer, and built on different lines, and could sail faster. They were smaller than our modern men-of-war, but carried more guns for their size. They were, as the Spaniards said, "very nimble and of good steerage, so that the English did with them as they desired. And our ships being very heavy compared with the lightness of those of the enemy, it was impossible to come to hand-stroke with them."

The English ships were manned with sailors and gunners who could both sail the ships and fight the enemy.

The guns were fired at the hulls of the Spanish ships and not wasted on the enemy's rigging, which was harder to aim at.

The fleets met on the 1st of July, and there followed a week of fighting and of disasters to the Spaniards. Yet as the news of their coming up the Channel came to those on shore, who watched beside the beacon fires with anxious hearts, the danger must have seemed little less fearful than before. Those who viewed the "greatness and hugeness of the Spanish army" from the sea, considered that the only way to move them was by fire-ships.

Sidonia had steered his great fleet magnificently through the dangers of the Channel; he anchored outside Calais to await the answer to the urgent messages he had sent to the Duke of Parma. But, as we know, the "Narrow Seas" were well watched by the English, and they were so helped by the Dutch that Parma never reached the shores of England.

Eight fire-ships were hastily prepared and sent down upon the Spanish fleet, "all burning fiercely. These worked great mischief among the Spanish ships (though none of them took fire), for in the panic their cables and anchors were slipped."

The great fight took place off Gravelines; on the Flemish coast, where most of the scattered ships of the Armada had drifted in the general confusion. The English hastened to take advantage of this confusion, while Sidonia was forming his fleet again into battle order. They "set upon the fleet of Spain (led by Sir Francis Drake in the *Revenge)* and gave them a sharp fight," while Lord Howard stopped to capture a helpless ship, the finest, they said, upon the sea. "And that day, Sir Francis' ship was riddled with every kind of shot."

The fight went on from nine in the morning till six at night, when the Spanish fleet bore away, beaten, towards the north. Howard says that "after the fight, notwithstanding that our powder and shot was well near all spent, we set on a brag-countenance and gave them chase as though we had wanted nothing (or lacked nothing) until we had cleared our own coast and some part of Scotland of them."

Drake was appointed to follow the fleet, and he writes, "We have the army of Spain before us, and mind, with the grace of God, to wrestle a pull with him. There was never anything pleased me better than seeing the enemy flying with a southerly wind to the northwards. God grant you have a good eye to the Duke of Parma: for with the grace of God, if we live, I doubt it not but ere it be long so to handled the matter with the Duke of Sidonia as he shall wish himself at St. Mary Port among his orange trees."

At the end of this letter he says, "I crave pardon of your honour for my haste, for that I had to watch this last night upon the enemy." And in another letter to Walsingham he signs himself, "Your honour's most ready to be commanded but now half-sleeping Francis Drake."

Many of the Spanish ships, being so crippled, were wrecked in stormy weather off the coasts of Scotland

and Ireland, which were unknown to them, and thus the more dangerous. Not half of those who put out to sea ever reached Spain again. Many men were killed in battle or died of their wounds, and they were the most fortunate, for others were drowned, or perished miserably by the hands of the natives of the coasts. Some who escaped were put to death by the Queen's orders, and some lingered in the foul prisons of that time. The instinct of savage cruelty revives, even in highly civilized races, in time of war, and spreads, like an infection.

We get a glimpse, in an old list of plunder taken from the Spanish prisoners, of the brave looks of the vanished host, that included the flower of Spanish youth and chivalry. There were "breeches and jerkins of silk, and hose of velvet, all laid over with gold lace, a pair of breeches of yellow satin, drawn out with cloth of silver, a leather jerkin, perfumed with amber and laid over with a gold and silver lace, a jerkin embroidered with flowers, and a blue stitched taffety hat, with a silver band and a plume of feathers."

For some time England was haunted by fears that the Armada would return to her coasts, or that Parma would avenge himself. But the reports of the many wrecks and of the massacre of Spanish soldiers eased this present anxiety. And it was well, for fever and sickness broke out in the English ships, and the men were dying in hundreds, "sickening one day and dying the next," as the letters say. The ships had to be disinfected and many of the men dispersed.

FIGHTING THE GREAT ARMADA.

Expedition to Lisbon

The great Armada was scattered, and yet the English did not feel secure from their enemy. The sight of that fleet so near their shores in "its terror and majesty," and the memory of its vast army of well-drilled soldiers, left a feeling of deep uneasiness in the minds of wise men. "Sir," writes Howard to Walsingham, "safe bind, safe find. A kingdom is a great wager. Sir, you know security is dangerous: and had God not been our best friend, we should have found it so. Some made little account of the Spanish force by sea: but I do warrant you, all the world never saw such a force as theirs was...."

Fortune had favoured England this time, but what if Philip built newer and lighter ships, and really succeeded in landing his army? They did not as yet know that Philip had no money to build his ships with, and rumours of a second invasion were plentiful.

The Spaniards, it is true, had suffered great loss and a crushing defeat to their pride, but they had not, after all, lost anything that they already had, but only failed to get something they wanted very badly to have, and the second kind of loss matters far less than the first.

But, on the other hand, if the English had been defeated,

it is difficult to think how darkly their history might have been changed. It was this thought that made the wise men sober in the midst of the national joy and exultation. They saw how much England, as an island, must depend for strength and defence upon her navy, and they saw this much more clearly than before. But Drake had seen it for a long time. And he had seen something more. He had seen that the English navy must be ready and able to protect her merchant ships by distressing and attacking her enemies abroad, and that this was a means of keeping the enemy so busy abroad that he could not invade the peace of England at home.

Elizabeth was eager to complete the destruction of Philip's navy, now so much crippled. In the spring of 1589 she consented to a new expedition being fitted out, and appointed Sir John Norreys and Sir Francis Drake as commanders-in-chief. The two men had fought together in Ireland. "Black John Norreys," as he was called, came of a famous fighting family, and had served in the Lowlands and in France with high courage and skill. During the Spanish invasion he had been made chief of the land forces. It is said that in one battle he went on fighting after three horses had been killed under him. With him went his brother Edward, and a famous Welsh captain, Sir Roger Williams, was his second is command.

The objects of the expedition were: first, to distress the King of Spain's ships; second, to get possession of some of the islands of the Azores in order to waylay the treasure ships; and, lastly, to try to recover for Don Antonio his lost kingdom of Portugal.

Money for this expedition was raised from every possible source. The Queen gave six royal ships and two pinnaces, money, food, and arms. The forces were made up of soldiers, gentlemen who wished to make their fortunes in war, and English and Dutch sailors and recruits, most of whom were pressed. With this large but mixed army the generals prepared to face the best-trained soldiers in Europe.

As usual, there were many delays. The Ships were not ready to go out, and much of the food was consumed before they started. More was not to be had, though Drake and Norreys wrote letter after letter begging for supplies. The Queen had already begun to regard the expedition with disfavour. Some days before the fleet sailed, the young Earl of Essex, her latest Court favourite, had slipped away to sea with Sir Roger Williams on the *Swiftsure*. He was tired of a courtier's life, and wanted to breathe freer air, and to help to fight the Spaniards. The Queen was very angry, and sent orders for his arrest, accusing Drake and Norreys of aiding his escape. But they declared they knew nothing of his plans.

About this time some Flemish ships appeared in Plymouth harbour laden with barley and wine, and Drake seized their cargoes in the Queen's name to victual his fleet, and sailed early in April. The weather was so rough that several of the ships containing troops were unable to get beyond the Channel, but even with lesser numbers the crews were short of food before they reached Spain.

Philip was very ill at this time, and in grave anxiety. He knew that Drake and the English ships might land on his coasts, that the French might cross the mountains with an invading force, and that the Portuguese might arise in rebellion to win back the crown for Don Antonio. This last danger seemed to Philip the most urgent, and Drake guessed this, and landed his men on the north-west coast at Corunna.

In doing this he tried to obey the Queen's orders to distress the King's ships, and also, no doubt, to satisfy the craving of his hungry crews for food and plunder. The lower town of Corunna was taken, and much wine and food consumed and much wasted. The townsfolk were routed and put to the sword, and their houses burned. An attempt to take the upper town failed, but the English were the victors in a sharp battle which took place some miles from the town, and they thus secured their retreat to the ships and sailed away.

The presence of Drake on the coasts caused great panic, for his name and luck had become a terror to the people. Philip felt deeply insulted that such an attack should be made "by a woman, mistress of half an island, with the help of a pirate and a common soldier." In Spain, as we have seen, the command was always given to gentlemen of high birth and breeding and title.

Four days after leaving Corunna, the fleet first sighted

some of the missing ships, and also the *Swiftsure* with the missing Earl, who had "put himself into the journey against the opinion of the world, and, as it seemed, to the hazard of his great fortune." The *Swiftsure* had taken six prizes off Cape St. Vincent.

The two generals had from the first wished to go straight to Lisbon, and it is thought that if they had done so, and thus given the Spaniards no warning of their coming, they might have had success. But they were hindered by the Queen's orders to destroy the shipping now collected in the northern ports, and chiefly in Santander. After leaving Corunna, however, they decided in council not to attempt that port, both soldiers and sailors reasoning that the conditions did not favour an attack.

They landed next at the Portuguese town of Peniche, which lies about fifty miles north of Lisbon. It was difficult to land on the surf-bound coast, and some of the boats were upset and battered. At last, Essex sprang into the waves and waded ashore with his soldiers and climbed the steep cliffs. The commandant, thus surprised, willingly surrendered to Antonio as his lawful king. "The king" soon had a following of peasants and friars, but neither nobles nor soldiers came to help him. He was eager to march to Lisbon, where he thought he was sure of a welcome. Norreys resolved to march there overland. Drake, it is said, would have liked better to attack the town from the sea in his usual daring but successful fashion. But the soldiers' plan carried the day; and leaving some ships at Peniche, Drake promised, if he could, to bring the fleet to meet them at Cascaes, at the mouth of the river Tagus, south of Lisbon.

There, when he arrived, he waited, not liking to venture up the river without knowing where the soldiers were, and not liking to quit the sea, where he could give them the means of retreat if necessary. For this he was very much blamed by the soldiers at the time, and afterwards when he got home. The point is still disputed.

Meanwhile the army was encamped outside the walls of Lisbon, but they never got inside. The Portuguese refused to join Don Antonio's party, and the Spanish governor kept the gates shut in a grim and heroic defence. The English sailors were sick and hungry; they had had no exercise on board ship to keep them healthy, and were exhausted with the heat. The stores and guns were on the ships with Drake. So, reluctantly, they left the suburbs of Lisbon and marched to Cascaes, where they embarked, not without some loss, and sailed away.

While they were still disputing in the councils, a fleet of German ships were sighted, and most of them secured. They were carrying corn and stores to Spain, against the rules of war, which bind countries not concerned in the quarrel to help neither foe. So the English seized sixty ships and the stores, both of which had been destined to furnish the new Armada of Spain.

Next came into view some English ships with supplies, but also with angry letters from the Queen; in answer to which Essex was sent home bearing the news that the expedition, though diminished by sickness and death, still meant to sail to the Azores.

On June the 8th a wind had scattered the fleet, and suddenly left it becalmed. The Lisbon galleys came out and cut off four English ships.

The winds continued to prevent the fleet from going towards the Azores, and all this time hundreds of sick and wounded men were dying. After seventeen days at sea, they landed at the town of Vigo and burned it, and laid waste the country round. At length storms and sickness and ill-fortune drove them home, and the expedition, woefully shrunken, straggled miserably back. Don Antonio died, poor and forsaken, some years later. The English had done a considerable amount of damage, but at great cost to themselves; for the loss of life was terrible, and that of money very considerable. Both Norreys and Drake were called upon to account for their failure, and at the time Drake got the most of the blame. Perhaps he was more hardly judged because failure had never come near him before, and his successes had always been so brilliant. His best friends at Court were dead, and for five years he was not asked to act in the Queen's service. So five years of his life which should have been the most active were spent in retirement, if not actually in "disgrace with fortune and men's eyes."

The war was carried on upon the old lines of distressing the King's ships, but with very poor success. After

Drake's voyage round the world, which encouraged other adventurers and treasure-seekers, the Spanish treasure-fleet had been carefully guarded. This was done by strongly fortifying the coast stations, by providing an armed escort, and a service of light ships, which went frequently to and fro with letters of advice and warning from the Indies to Spain.

Drake had ruined this defence in 1585, and in 1588 again many of the guard-ships had to be used in the service of the Armada. A really strong English fleet might at this time have stayed the treasure, but Philip continued to gather in his gold, and also began, with splendid patience, to rebuild his navy. In 1591 a royal squadron was sent out under Lord Thomas Howard, and the great battle of Sir Richard Grenville on the *Revenge* was fought, "the fight of the one and the fifty-three," with the loss of that ship and the victory of the Spanish fleet. The Queen made a fighting alliance with Henry the Fourth of France, who was the enemy of Philip, and this she felt would help to keep him out of England. Philip was now trying to establish a fortified station on the north coast of Brittany, from which his new Armada might be despatched.

THE LAST VOYAGE

Drake had settled in Buckland Abbey, which he had bought from Sir Richard Grenville. He helped to prepare and furnish ships for some of the different excursions against Spain, and he spent much time on schemes to improve Plymouth. He paid to have pure water brought to the town from many miles away; he had flour-mills built, that the sailors might have good biscuits provided for them, and he overlooked the work of fortifying Plymouth, and making it in all ways a strong naval Station.

As the danger of a fresh invasion by Philip grew more threatening, Drake was called to Court again, and it was about this time that he gave to the Queen his written story of the voyage to Nombre de Dios.

In 1595 a fresh expedition was arranged for the Indies, and after the usual bewildering indecision at Court, and difference of views and plans (delays that proved fatal to an excursion whose proper nature was to be swift and secret, and above all things powerful), on August 28, 1598, Sir Francis Drake started on his last voyage.

The story of the expedition begins by saying that "the Spaniard leaves no means untried to turn the peace of England into a cursed thraldom, and this is shown by his attempts, and also by his greedy desires to be our neighbour in Brittany, to gain so near us a quiet and safe road for his fleet. So the forces were sent to invade him in that kingdom from whence he has feathers to fly to the top of his high desires.

"The invasion was glorious spoken of long before it was sent, and Sir Francis Drake was named General. For his very name was a great terror to all in those parts, and he had done many things in those countries to his honourable fame and profit. But entering into them as the Child of Fortune, it may be that his self-willed and peremptory (despotic) command was doubted, and that caused her Majesty, as it should seem, to join Sir John Hawkins as second in command. He was an old, wary man, and so leaden-footed" (or slow in action) "that Drake's meat would be eaten before his was cooked. They were men of such different natures that what one desired the other commonly opposed. The journey had so glorious a name that crowds of volunteers came to them, and they had to discharge such few as they had pressed. Yet many times it was very doubtful if the voyage would be made, till at last the news came of a ship of the King of Spain, which was driven into Puerto Rico with two millions and a half of treasure. So her Majesty commanded them to haste their departure, which they did with twenty-seven ships."

The generals began to disagree soon after. Drake wanted to begin with an attack upon the Canaries, and Hawkins thought it unnecessary and unwise; and, as the story says, "the fire which lay hidden in their stomachs began to break forth."

It was five years since Drake had fought with his old enemies. He did not know how much stronger the Spanish defence at sea had become, owing to the lessons he had given them, nor how complete Philip had made the protection of the traffic and the treasure-ships. He was to see this first at the Canary Islands, where he tried, and failed, to make one of his old surprise visits.

The fleet sailed on, and anchored on the 29th of October, for water, at Guadeloupe. The *Delight* was the last of the ships to arrive the next day, and she brought news that the *Francis*, a small ship of the company, was taken by five Spanish ships, which had been sent out by Philip to bring home the wrecked ship at Puerto Rico. This was a great misfortune, because Sir John Hawkins had made known to all the company, "even to the basest mariners" the places whither they were bound, naming Puerto Rico, Nombre de Dios, and Panama. Now the Spaniards would learn this from their prisoners, and at once send warning to the coasts.

Drake wanted to give chase at once, but Hawkins was old and cautious, and desired to stay and mount his guns, take in water, set up his pinnaces, and make all things ready to meet the Spaniards.

And Sir John prevailed, "for that he was sickly, Sir Francis being loath to breed his further disquiet." It took four days to make those preparations, and always the sickness of Sir John increased. On the 12th of October Drake brought the fleet up by a secret way to Puerto Rico, and about three o'clock that afternoon Sir John Hawkins died.

In the evening, as Drake sat at supper, his chair was shot from under him, and two of his officers received their death wounds from the Spanish guns. The ships had to move away. The next night the English made a desperate effort to fire the five ships that had come for the treasure. Four of them were set alight, but only one was burnt, and by the great light she gave the Spaniards "played upon the English with their ordinance and small shot as if it had been fair day," and sunk some of the boats.

Next day Drake, undaunted by failure, determined to try and take his whole fleet boldly into the harbour and storm the place. But the Spaniards, guessing his desperate intention, and fearing his great courage, sunk four ships laden with merchandise and armed, as they were, and so, at a great sacrifice, blocked the way for the English.

Drake took counsel with the soldiers as to the strength of the place, but most of them thought it too great a risk, though one or two were for trying it. "The General presently said: 'I will bring you to twenty places far more wealthy and easier to be gotten;' and hence we went on the 15th. And here," says the teller of the story, "I left all hope of good success."

On the way to Nombre de Dios they stopped at Rio de la Hacha, where Drake had first been wronged by the

Spaniards. This town they took with little difficulty and some treasure was won.

On December 27th they were at Nombre de Dios, which they took with small resistance. But the people had been warned, and had fled and hidden their treasure, and the town was left very bare. So they resolved to "hasten with speed to Panama." The soldiers were under the command of Sir Thomas Baskerville, who had been a brave fighter against the Spaniards before now in Holland and France. They started to go to Panama by the old road well known to Drake. He, meanwhile, stayed with the ships and burned the town. He was about to sail nearer the river when news came that the soldiers were returning. The road was only too strongly defended now, and Baskerville's men were driven back with severe loss. They were a small force, and weak with the long march through heavy rains; their powder was wet and their food scarce and sodden, and Baskerville decided upon a retreat. "This march," says the story, "had made many swear that they would never buy gold at such a price again."

Drake, being disappointed of his highest hopes, now called a council to decide what was to be done. All the towns had been forewarned, and told "to be careful and look well to themselves, for that Drake and Hawkins were making ready in England to come upon them." And now the company seem to have regarded their leader with some bitterness, as his brave promises failed, and the places that he used to know were found to be changed and formidable. Now they had to rely "upon cards and maps, he being at these parts at the farthest limit of his knowledge." But still he proposed fresh places that had the golden sound of riches in their names, and gallant Baskerville said he would attempt both, one after another.

But the winds drove them instead to a "waste island, which is counted the sickliest place in the Indies, and there died many of the men, and victuals began to grow scarce. Here," says Maynarde, who writes the story, "I was often private with our General, and I demanded of him why he so often begged me, being in England, to stay with him in these parts as long as himself... He answered me with grief, protesting that he was as ignorant of the Indies as myself; and that he never thought any place could be so changed, as it were, from a delicious and pleasant arbour into a waste and desert wilderness: besides the variableness and changes of the wind and weather, so stormy and blustrous as he never saw it before. But he most wondered that since his coming out of England he never saw sail worth giving chase unto. Yet, in the greatness of his mind, he would, in the end, conclude with these words: 'It matters not, man; God hath many things in store for us. And I know many means to do her Majesty good service and to make us rich, for we must have gold before we reach England.'

"And since our return from Panama he never carried mirth nor joy in his face, yet no man he loved must show he took thought thereof. And he began to grow sickly. And now so many of the company were dying of the sickness, and food was getting so scarce, that at last he resolved 'to depart and take the wind as God sent it.'"

But the lurking fever in the swamp had done its work, and on January 28, 1596, after a brief fight with illness and death, Drake "yielded up his spirit like a Christian to his Creator quietly in his cabin."

"The General being dead," we are told, "most men's hearts were bent to hasten for England as soon as they might. 'Fortune's Child,' they said, 'was dead; things would not fall into their mouths, nor riches be their portions, how dearly soever they adventured for them.'

But Sir Thomas Baskerville assumed the command and took the remains of the fleet in his charge, and did not return home till he had met the Spaniards and fought a battle with them at sea.

Before the fleet left Puerto Rico he burned that port, and sunk two of the ships no longer needed, and all the prizes. And, there, a league from the shore, under seas, he left the body of Sir Francis Drake, heavily freighted with death and silence. But I like to think that his soul went a-roving again among the stars.

www.ingramcontent.com/pod-product-compliance
Lightning Source LLC
Chambersburg PA
CBHW031007210726
48290CB00007B/2512